DATE DUE

NOV 0 9 2022	
	PRINTED IN U.S.A.

The Disappearing Mr. Jacques

WRITTEN BY **GIDEON STERER** ★ ILLUSTRATED BY **BENJAMIN CHAUD**

Alfred A. Knopf 🐎 New York

Ladies and gentlemen,
boys and girls . . .

Look at me.

I am the astonishing, bewildering,
disappearing Mr. Jacques,
and my show has already begun.

Perhaps you have seen magic before . . .

A rabbit from a hat . . .

Scarves from a sleeve . . .

But with such tricks I will not waste your time.

What you are about to witness is magic more mysterious,

a performance most peculiar,

a marvel of mischief

that will require your full attention,

and both unblinking eyes.

Look at me . . .

while you still can.

Look at my
beautiful buttons,

my magnificent mustache,

my twirling timepiece,

my velvety vest.

Look closely, and remember
what you see,

for now I am fading. . . .

Yes, I am fading. . . .

And now . . .

and now . . .

I am gone.

But I am not *completely* gone.

You can still hear my voice, can't you?
And as I leave this book,
you will hear my footsteps, too.

Tip-tap.

Tip-tap.

Tip-tap.

Can you find me?
I'll give you a hint.

I am *very* close.
Am I behind you?
Am I beside you?

Am I . . .
perched atop your head?

Not anymore.

Watch this space.
Do not look away,
for now I'm coming back.

Now . . .

Don't worry. No one finds me on the first try.
But how, you are wondering, can a man of such
presence simply disappear?
Where could such elegant boots walk off to?
How could such a handsome face hide?

I have labored a lifetime to learn these
secrets and more.
I am quick enough to blur,

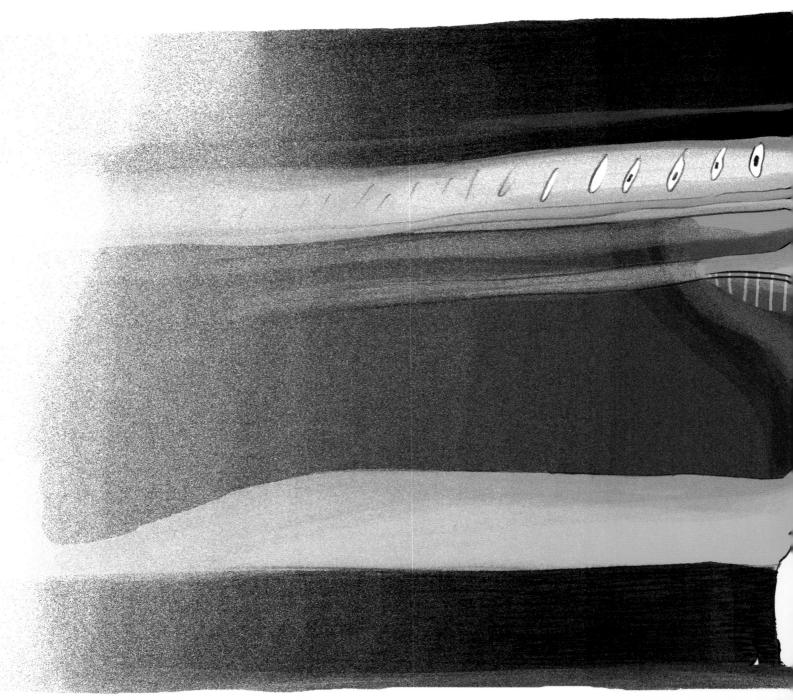

wiggly enough to wedge,
and dainty enough to drape across the pages of a book.

I have dazzled dukes and duchesses,
stupefied kings and queens,
but now
I perform for you here.
On the page . . .

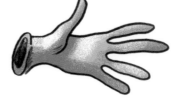

and off.

Perhaps, given another chance,
you will find me.

Allow me to be more bold. . . .

Hold out your hand.

Make a fist.

I will reappear inside your hand . . .

but if you open it, I will vanish.

Do you not believe me?

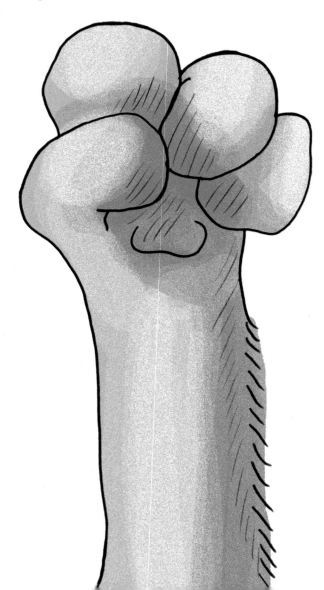

Is your hand getting warmer?
I think so.
It's dark in here.
And too hot to wear a hat.

Open your hand. . . .

Did you see my coattails fly?

Maybe it would help if I made some noise. . . .

THRUMP—THRUMP—THRUMP.

I roll across the floor.

My mother-of-pearl cane goes

TAP-TAP

on your window.

I waltz on walls, PIT-PAT-PIT.

S l i d e

across the ceiling,

SWISH-

SWASH-

SWISH,

and leap in silence . . .

. . . to land upon your nose!

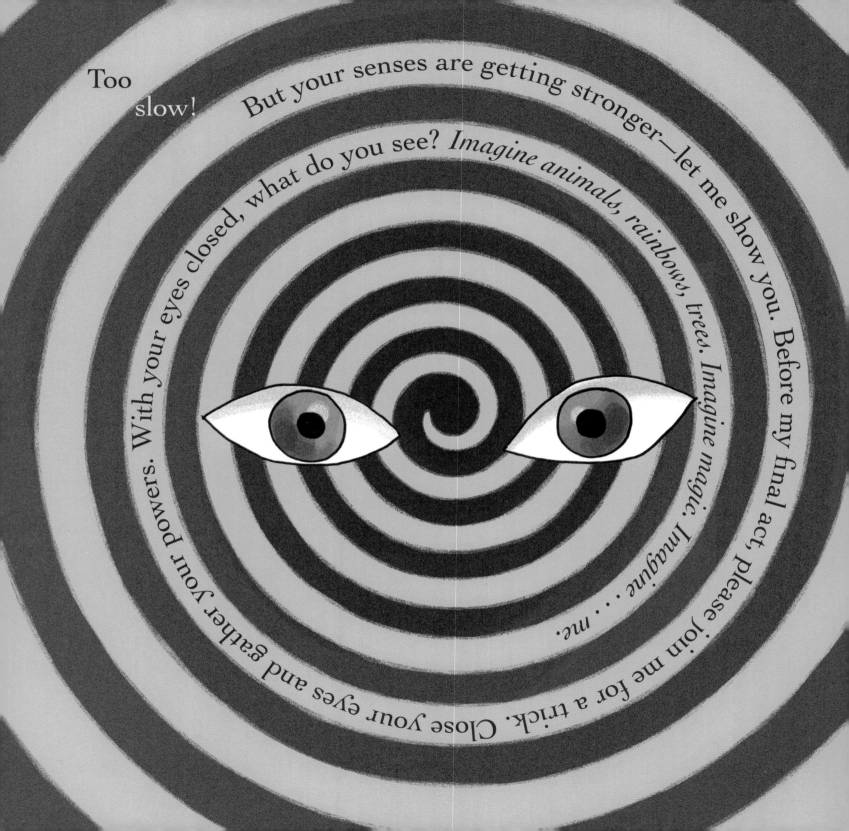

Too slow! But your senses are getting stronger—let me show you. Before my final act, please join me for a trick. Close your eyes and gather your powers. With your eyes closed, what do you see? Imagine animals, rainbows, trees. Imagine magic. Imagine . . . me.

Now, for a moment, take this book and wear it
on your head, like this.

Brilliant! Do you see what you've done?

Indeed, it seems *you* could be a magician. . . .

So with my final trick, I will make you a deal:
if you find me, I will teach *you* how to disappear,
just as I have taught my rabbit.

Look at our buttons,
our mustaches,
our vests.

Yes, look closely, and remember
what you see. . . .

For now we are fading . . .

Yes, we are fading . . .

and now . . .

and now . . .

we are gone.

Tap-tap

Swish-swish

Ta-ta.

For my dear friend, Michael A. Caccio—ever a master showman
—G.S.

For Alex, the magician
—B.C.

THIS IS A BORZOI BOOK PUBLISHED BY ALFRED A. KNOPF

Text copyright © 2022 by Gideon Sterer
Jacket art and interior illustrations copyright © 2022 by Benjamin Chaud

All rights reserved. Published in the United States by Alfred A. Knopf,
an imprint of Random House Children's Books, a division of Penguin Random House LLC, New York.

Knopf, Borzoi Books, and the colophon are registered trademarks of Penguin Random House LLC.

Visit us on the Web! rhcbooks.com

Educators and librarians, for a variety of teaching tools, visit us at RHTeachersLibrarians.com

Library of Congress Cataloging-in-Publication Data is available upon request.
ISBN 978-0-525-57941-0 (trade) — ISBN 978-0-525-57942-7 (lib. bdg.) — ISBN 978-0-525-57943-4 (ebook)

The text of this book is set in Cochin.
The illustrations were created using gray pencil and digital color.
Book design by Nicole de las Heras

MANUFACTURED IN CHINA
August 2022
10 9 8 7 6 5 4 3 2 1

First Edition